SUSAN LEHR

Tania's Trolls

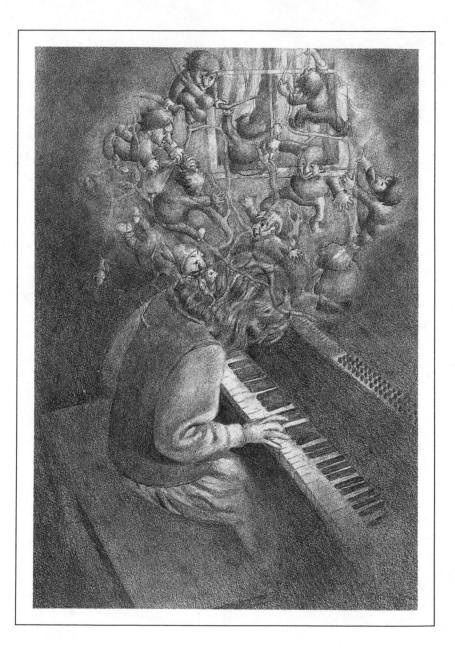

Tania's Trolls

By Lisa Westberg Peters
Illustrated by Sharon Wooding

Arcade Publishing • *New York*

Little, Brown and Company

PZ
7
P44174
TaN
1989

For Magna Diderikke Monson Westberg

Text copyright © 1989 by Lisa Westberg Peters
Illustrations copyright © 1989 by Sharon Wooding
ALL RIGHTS RESERVED
No part of this book may be reproduced in any form or by any electronic or
mechanical means, including information storage and retrieval systems, without
permission in writing from the publisher, except by a reviewer who may quote
brief passages in a review.
FIRST EDITION

The characters and events in this book are fictitious. Any similarity to real persons,
living or dead, is coincidental and not intended by the author.

Library of Congress Cataloging-in-Publication Data
Peters, Lisa Westberg.
    Tania's trolls / by Lisa Westberg Peters; illustrated by Sharon
Wooding. — 1st ed.
        p.   cm.
    Summary: a formidable grandmother helps young Tania overcome
her stage fright.
    ISBN 1-55970-040-8
    [1. Grandmothers — Fiction.]   1. Wooding, Sharon, ill.   11. Title.
    PZ7.P44174TAN   1989
    [Fic] — dc20   89-38443
                                                          CIP
                                                          AC

Published in the United States by
Arcade Publishing, Inc., New York, a Little, Brown company

10 9 8 7 6 5 4 3 2 1

HC

Published simultaneously in Canada by
Little, Brown and Company (Canada) Limited
PRINTED IN THE UNITED STATES OF AMERICA

Contents

Tania's Trolls

Inga

Tania ran across the grimy floor of the train depot, her footsteps echoing off the bare walls. She eagerly pressed her nose against a window to look down the track.

"Where is it? Is her train late?"

Coming up beside her, her father said, "Nope, here it comes."

Tania looked again. There it was, just a dot of light, a low rumble. As the train approached, the dot of light turned into a blinding white eye, the rumble into a thundering roar. In the black March night, the train seemed more like a monster.

Tania jumped at the screaming whistle that announced, unnecessarily, the train's arrival.

"Wow," said Eric, watching the engine as it slowed and finally stopped. "Trains are great."

Tania nodded. "I can't wait to see Grandma."

When the old woman finally stepped out of the coach, Tania sucked in her breath. Grandma Inga looked much older. But it had been years since Tania had seen her.

Her grandmother even looked shorter, but Tania figured that was partly because she herself had grown. Now Grandma Inga was only a little taller than she was.

Tania's father ran ahead to carry her suitcase. As soon as Grandma Inga caught sight of him, she began talking, frowning, gesturing all at once. She pulled at her dress in front and then searched for something in a big black purse.

"It's my stomach," Tania heard her complain. "And I can't seem to put my hands on that medicine."

Her grandmother's obvious bad mood made Tania slow down and stop. Eric stopped, too.

"Hi, Grandma," Tania called out in a small voice, suddenly feeling shy.

"Hi, Grandma," Eric said.

She must not have heard. She kept digging in her purse.

"You know, John," she persisted. "It was just terrible. I didn't sleep a wink. And the service. My stars."

"I know," said Tania's father. "Trains aren't what they used to be. Come on now, Mother. Look who came along." He turned and grinned at Tania and Eric.

"Hi, Grandma," Tania said again and smiled.

Grandma Inga paused to take a long look at them. She hugged Eric and gave him a peck on the cheek. Then she hugged Tania.

In a rush, Tania felt relief wash over her. She instantly recognized the flowery perfume, the powdery, dry skin, and the soft cushion of her grandmother's embrace.

Now, now, Tania, everything will be all right. She could hear the words her grandmother used to say to her as a small child, and she waited to hear them again.

Instead, Grandma Inga held Tania at arm's length and asked, "So . . . are you ready for your big piano festival? Are you practicing hard?"

Tania laughed. "Sure, aren't I, Dad?" The piano festival was just a week away, at the end of spring break.

"Tania practices harder than anyone I know," her father said.

"All the time," agreed Eric.

"Well, that's what it takes," said Grandma Inga. "John, I've got to find that stomach medicine. I'm in such pain."

Then she stopped again to look at Tania. "I understand from your father's letters that things didn't go very well at the Christmas recital. What happened?"

Tania cringed at the thought of the horrid recital. Her mind had filled up with everything but the music, and she had skipped whole sections of the song.

"I guess I was pretty nervous," Tania said.

Grandma Inga showed no sign of wanting to get into the car. "What's there to be afraid of?" she asked. "It's an honor to perform. It's what a musician lives for. John, does she still have Mrs. Helgeson for a teacher?"

"Yes, of course."

"Well," Grandma Inga declared, "she's good. Not too . . . *gentle* with the young ones . . . but then, you aren't so little anymore, are you, Tania? Were you unprepared? You can't go up there unprepared, you know. That's the key. Preparation."

Tania looked to her father for help and he winked. Then he pulled at his mother's arm. "We can talk about this later. We'll find that stomach medicine when we get home. You need to feel good to make lefse tomorrow or it won't turn out."

"Lefse!" said Grandma Inga. "I tell you, I can't make good lefse anymore. I'm too old."

"Nonsense," said Tania's father.

Tania watched them get into the car.

Now, now, Tania, everything will be all right. She'll tell me later, Tania thought, when she's not so tired.

After everyone had gone to bed, Tania stayed downstairs. Her cat, Dodger, jumped onto her lap.

Tania stroked him, but her eyes were on the photograph of her grandmother. It had sat on top of the piano for as long as she could remember.

Grandma Inga had been Tania's first piano teacher. Even after she moved, she always wrote and asked how Tania was doing with her music.

"I didn't tell her," Tania whispered to Dodger. Dodger's ears flicked at the sound. "She'd have a fit."

But to the photograph, Tania whispered, "I might quit piano, Grandma." It wasn't the music or the long

5

hours of practice. She loved the music and she loved to play.

It was the performing she feared. And it seemed to be getting harder, not easier, for her.

Her friend Jo had said last week, "Too bad your grandma can't go to the festival and play it for you."

Tania had agreed. But she knew her grandmother would find a way to help. Grandma Inga was good. Very good. She could play the piano with her eyes closed.

Lap Concerts

Tania set Dodger on the piano keys. The cat plunked out a few accidental chords, then leaped to his usual spot on top of the piano.

"OK, OK, I'll practice," she said. She played a series of chords and scales to warm up her fingers and her mind for harder things.

Then she practiced her festival song. In a way, the song was simple. It started low, slow, and soft, but it gradually climbed in every way — pitch, tempo, and volume.

By now, Tania knew it inside out. In fact, Mrs. Helgeson had told her once to memorize it backwards, phrase by phrase, to get it firmly into her mind.

Tania had done that. Still, she was afraid of panicking. Panic would undo everything.

"I didn't know you were playing a *Peer Gynt* piece for the festival," Grandma Inga said, lowering herself into the rocking chair. "Troll music." Then she chuckled. "That sounds like you."

Tania grinned. She had grown up on her grandmother's troll stories. When she was little, she had believed that trolls lived in the big oak tree outside her bedroom window. She used to imagine that they could climb up the branches at night, dance in the moonlight, and sing wild and scary music.

Even now, she would pull her bedroom window curtains shut a little more quickly if the sky was already black.

"I'm having trouble," Tania told her grandmother, "playing it fast enough at the end."

"I played that song once, years ago, while I was riding a train across the country," said Grandma Inga.

"You did?"

"I certainly did," her grandmother said. "The lounge car had a piano. I had played for quite a while when I noticed the sunset through the windows. Big puffy clouds, all red and gold and orange. They reminded me of mountains, like the mountains of Norway."

Tania reached for Dodger and held him in her lap. She could feel a story coming on.

"So I played the mountain troll song," Grandma Inga said. "And when I got to the end, all the crashing and carrying-on, I looked out again and the clouds had spread over the entire sky. Deep purple they were."

Tania stared. "Wow. It must have seemed like magic."

"It did."

"Well," said Tania, turning back to face the piano

keys, "I doubt if I'll be making any magic Saturday. I'll be lucky if I make it to the end of the song."

Grandma Inga got up out of her chair. "Did I hear a bad key, right around here?" She played a few notes.

"There it is. Tell your pa to get that fixed. I remember the piano at the Dahlstroms' house — this was way out in western North Dakota. One key on it was terrific. It had all the notes in one, I think.

"I opened up the piano and I just tied the hammer to the strings with yarn so it wouldn't sound at all. You couldn't just call up a piano tuner out there in those days."

"I'll remind Dad," Tania promised.

"And Tania," her grandmother continued, "isn't this how fast your festival piece is supposed to be played?" Grandma Inga reached in front of her and played a snatch of the song about twice as fast as Tania had ever played it.

Tania felt confused as her grandmother hovered over her and offered bits of advice. She wanted help from her. Now she was getting it, and it didn't feel right. It didn't feel the way it used to feel.

"Tania! Inga! Come on, we're almost ready to make lefse." It was her mother in the kitchen.

Tania nearly leaped away from the piano.

Making lefse with Grandma Inga was always a busy, messy time. Lots of singing, laughing, and rolling the lefse into animal shapes instead of plain old circles.

9

And the best part was eating the paper-thin pastries with melted butter while they were still warm.

Grandma Inga followed Tania into the kitchen and wrapped a big white towel around her middle. She tested the temperature of the silver griddle with a quick swipe of her finger. A bottle of pills lay on the counter next to her purse.

Good, thought Tania. Grandma Inga had found her medicine.

Her mother was stacking thick towels on the table. Her father was filing down the end of a thin stick that would be used for flipping lefse.

"Can I flip one, Grandma?" Eric asked, as he spread a half-inch of strawberry jam on a piece of toast.

"Sure," Grandma Inga said.

Tania patted the small ball of potato dough with flour. Then she rolled it out gently. "I think this one looks a little like a . . . hippo!" she declared. "Don't you, Eric?"

Eric peered at it. "It looks like a *sick* hippo."

Tania laughed and poked him with her rolling pin.

Grandma Inga carefully lifted the lefse with the stick and set it on the hot griddle to cook. "I remember Mother making lefse on the wood stove. It was beautiful lefse. It's all in the potatoes. North Dakota potatoes are the best, you know. They're drier."

Eric grabbed the bag and examined it. "These are from Idaho."

She handed him the stick. Eric jabbed it under the

lefse and flipped. The lefse landed in a crumpled heap and sizzled.

"Yuck!" Tania squealed. "You get to eat that one, Eric."

Grandma Inga flipped the next one cleanly. She shook her dish-towel apron, and flour flew. Tania's mother winced at the white cloud. Everyone else laughed.

"Mother taught me everything," Grandma Inga went on. "She taught me how to cook, how to sew. She taught me how to play the piano when I was only three. She taught all of us kids, all eight."

Grandma Inga took the lefse off the griddle and set it carefully between two thick towels. "Mother was much stricter with me than I was with you, Tania."

Piano lessons with Grandma Inga hadn't been like real lessons. She hadn't worried about teaching things in the right order. And she never even used regular piano books. The lessons came straight from her long fingers and from the stacks of sheet music she had given to Tania's family.

"Remember the animal scale songs, Grandma?" Tania asked. " 'A' was an acrobatic aardvark doing three sharp somersaults."

Grandma Inga smiled. "And 'F'?"

" 'F' was a fat frog with one flat tongue," Tania answered without hesitating. They both laughed.

"I can't remember all of them," Tania admitted.

Grandma Inga shook her head. "Neither can I."

Tania began rolling out another ball of dough. The best part of those lessons had been when Tania grew tired. Her grandmother would scoop her onto her lap and play a private concert.

Tania had loved sitting on her grandmother's soft lap and breathing in her flowery perfume. It was like hearing a bedtime story.

Grandma Inga lifted another piece of lefse with her stick.

"But I can't teach you how to perform, Tania," she said. "You just have to *know* that. You used to be able to perform when you were little. What happened?"

Tania's rolling pin stopped.

It was true. Performing hadn't always bothered her. The times she had performed for relatives or friends, she had never noticed the others much.

As she got older, she became more aware of the eyes watching, the ears listening. Her music was no longer a cozy, private hour on her grandmother's lap.

Tania stood the rolling pin on its end and spun it around. "I don't know what happened. My mind goes blank. I'm so afraid of getting it wrong in front of all those people."

Please, Grandma, Tania thought, can you help me?

Grandma Inga shook her head as if she could read Tania's mind. "I don't know about nervousness on the stage. I never had it."

Tania felt an invisible wall rising between them.

There was the reassuring grandmother in the picture on top of the piano, and in her memory. And then there was this grandmother.

Her mother broke in. "I don't think Tania's as outgoing as you are, Inga. We're trying not to push her too much."

Grandma Inga didn't say anything as she added another piece of lefse to the growing stack under the towels.

"By the way," Tania's mother added airily, "I hope you don't mind, Inga. We invited some of your old Minneapolis friends and cousins over tomorrow night to hear you play. We thought you'd be too tired today."

"Oh, heavens," Grandma Inga objected. "I didn't bring any good dresses, just the one for Tania's festival."

Tania slipped out of the kitchen and ran around the snow patches. She didn't want to hear any more.

She sat down behind the big oak tree and looked up. The tree's black branches were as bristly as an old man's whiskers. Pale green buds should have been popping out by now, but it was too cold. A slow spring. It was just another disappointment.

Monday

Grandma's Trolls

After dinner, Grandma Inga's friends and cousins started to arrive.

Tania smiled and let people in whether she recognized them or not. Most of the time she didn't. She decided that if they wore fake-fur coats and brown shoes, they were cousins. If they wore cloth coats and clunky black shoes, they were old buddies.

Somehow they all knew her.

"Hello, Tania," each one said, and held her arm tightly. A few asked, "How's your piano playing?" Another whispered, "You've got your grandmother's talent, you know."

Tania thanked them and said her piano playing was fine. It was too much trouble to say more than that.

In the living room, Grandma Inga held court. She was like royalty, drawing people and praise. "Inga, you look wonderful. That dry Phoenix climate must be good for you," someone said.

Tania watched it all. It was as if her grandmother were onstage already.

Finally Tania's mother must have decided that everyone had arrived. "Inga," she said, "you don't need any introductions. Play for us."

"I forgot my piano glasses upstairs, wouldn't you know?" Grandma Inga said as she approached the piano bench. "But you youngsters don't care if I get the notes right, do you?"

Everyone laughed.

Grandma Inga slid onto the bench. She adjusted her dress and peered down to find the pedals.

"You know, when I was sixteen," she said, "I was assistant organist at church, and I always arrived with a string of toddlers, my four youngest brothers and sisters."

Tania smiled. It made her grandmother sound like a mother duck leading a string of ducklings.

Grandma Inga looked around at the group. "Now I'm surrounded by gray hair."

Everyone laughed again.

Even before she was completely settled, Grandma Inga began to play. The music that came from the piano was not the sound of hammers pounding against strings inside an upright black box. It was the sound of water tumbling over a waterfall. Rushing and rich, it flowed into the room.

Tania was soon caught up by the beauty and magic of it. She stared at her grandmother's fingers floating over the keyboard. They spread confidently for full chords, then barely touched the keys for a more delicate sound.

Tania's glance shifted. Her grandmother's eyes

were closed. All this magic, and she wasn't even watching where her fingers went. How did she do that?

When Grandma Inga finished the piece, everyone clapped.

"That was beautiful, Inga," said Tania's mother.

"It was," said her father.

It was, thought Tania. But she didn't say it.

Grandma Inga played for a long time. In spite of herself, Tania wished she would never stop, but she finally did. Grandma Inga turned around on the bench and searched the room. Her eyes settled on Tania.

"And now, I'd like to hear our Tania. Come now. Play for us."

Tania felt herself go cold. Her chest tightened. This wasn't her day to play. Hers was five days from now. Wasn't that enough?

She moved an inch closer to her father and looked up at him. He just raised his eyebrows and shrugged. "Play an old one," he whispered. "One that you know real well."

Tania's mind raced desperately. She clasped her chair with her hands, which were already clammy with cold sweat. Thoughts of the Christmas recital bounced across her mind.

Finally, after what seemed like hours, she decided to play a song she'd learned earlier in the year. It wasn't hard.

"All right," she said. She stood up and saw that everyone was smiling at her — everyone except Grandma

Inga, who had slid off the bench and was chatting with one of her old friends.

At the piano, Tania wiped her sticky hands on her jeans. She stared at the keys. Each one seemed to be the face of an old man or old woman staring back at her.

She began. The music sounded faraway. Her hands felt detached from her arms. One measure, another measure. Soft here, loud there.

Then nothing. Nothing.

What was next? Tania fought a sudden urge to bolt from the room and run outside to her oak tree.

"Do you want to try it again?" a voice asked. "It might have been her mother, but Tania wasn't sure.

Tania did want to try again, but the music was gone — a simple song that she had known backward and forward. There was no applause at all. Tears didn't come. Tania felt only a lump in her throat.

As she returned to her chair, she caught a glimpse of Grandma Inga and the tiniest shake of her head.

Tania found it nearly impossible to swallow her grandmother's lefse. For the first time, it tasted like thick, dry cardboard.

No one talked about Tania's performance. Someone asked instead about her grandmother's health.

Grandma Inga shook her head. "Bad, bad. It's my stomach. Fussy these days. Can't eat anything. And my eyes are going. The doctor says he can't do anything for me."

19

"Has your finger given you any trouble lately?" someone else asked.

"What's that about your finger?" an old man asked.

"I thought everyone knew this story," Grandma Inga said. "My older brother Henry and I used to take the six younger ones sledding and skating on the Crooked Tail River. We would pour water on the bank the evening before, and by morning it was ice.

"We could slide quite a ways in the big wooden chopping bowl. I broke my collarbone once, and I think Hilda did, too. It was dangerous, but we loved it.

"And it was never smooth skating because the river froze while it was flowing. Once, when I was eleven or so, Henry skated right over my hand and nearly sliced off my little finger."

Tania felt her stomach roll, even though she had heard the story before.

"I held it in snow to keep it cold, and the doctor sewed it back on. It's almost as good as new, I tell you."

She held up her hand and wiggled her finger. All Tania could see was a faint white line. It looked nearly the same as her other little finger.

"Oh, it took me a while to be able to play the piano again," Grandma Inga said. "But nothing could keep me away."

Tania found herself staring at her own hands. She heard her grandmother launch into another story.

"Don't you remember, Sarah? The old church in Pleasanton, before they tore it down?"

Sarah nodded her head. "Of course," she said. "White clapboard, with a picket fence around it. I remember."

"My goodness, I'll never forget it," Grandma Inga went on. "I sang my first solo there. My older cousin had said, 'Inga, watch out for the trolls hiding in the back. They'll grab you if you sing sour.'"

A wave of goose bumps spread over Tania. *They'll grab you if you sing sour.* Would trolls grab you if you played the piano badly?

"I was too young," Grandma Inga was saying, "to know that trolls won't go into a church for anything. Anyway, I was so afraid of seeing a troll, I fell off the stage. But I climbed back on and sang three Christmas songs in Norwegian.

"I didn't take my eyes off the back of the stage. Nobody grabbed me, so I guess I sang all right. I was only three, mind you."

Tania groaned softly. She'd forgotten that part. How could a three-year-old sing when she thought trolls were going to grab her?

She sighed. Grandma Inga could.

I used to think Grandma and I were exactly alike, Tania thought, because we both loved music. But we're not. Give me a stage and I freeze up like ice.

Tuesday

Pretend Festival

Tania's friend Jo came over the next morning.
"Come on, shorty," she said. "Let's shoot some baskets
at my house."

Tania pulled on a sweatshirt. "OK, I'm ready."

"Is it nice to see your grandma?" Jo asked when
the door slammed behind them. She dribbled the basketball in front of her as she walked.

"Sort of," said Tania. "She played the piano yes-
terday with her eyes shut."

"She did?" Jo said. "I don't believe it."

"It's true."

Jo looked at Tania as if she expected more. Tania
didn't give her more.

"Must be something to see," Jo prompted.

"It is."

"All right. What happened?"

"I don't know!" Tania declared. "She's different,
meaner. I suppose I'm not much fun, either, because of
the festival. It's going to be judged and everything."

"Judged!" said Jo. "That makes you sound like a

criminal." She stopped dribbling her basketball, and they walked toward Jo's house silently.

Tania decided to tell Jo about her plan to quit piano if things went badly at the festival.

Jo didn't like it. "You'll get over it, Tania. I did. My first few basketball games, I was so nervous I threw air balls all the time. Home runs. I was so embarrassed. But now . . ." She paused to spin the ball on her finger. "I'm a star."

Tania laughed. "You know what I wish . . . I wish the festival could be at my house."

"Dream on. Your own private festival?"

"Yeah," said Tania. "With just Mom, Dad, Eric, Grandma, and you. Wouldn't it be great? I wouldn't be nearly as nervous. Maybe it would even be fun."

Jo slapped the ball into the basket behind her garage.

"Fun!" she declared. "That's it. Why don't we have a *pretend* festival at your house? It would be good practice for the real thing. I'll be Mrs. Helgeson. Eric can be the judge. It'll be a riot."

"Eric a judge?" Tania asked doubtfully.

"Sure," said Jo. "He'll love it. Let's do it this afternoon."

"OK. Why not?" Tania grabbed the ball from Jo and tried to make a shot, but it bounced off the backboard. Jo ran circles around her and made ten baskets in a row. Tania screamed that it was unfair, and insisted they make things more even.

So, for a while, Jo played with her eyes shut.

*   *   *

While she waited for Jo to arrive, Tania sat down at the piano. Instead of practicing, she stared out the window at the leftover winter.

"I can't wait till it warms up," she whispered.

A snatch of a melody flitted through her head. Her fingers soon found the melody on the piano. It started slowly, weaving back and forth like a child on a swing. Then it soared and touched the sky. A fresh spring breeze seemed to blow over her.

She hummed a simple harmony and then played, both hands together. She played it over and over like a child pumping higher and higher.

The doorbell finally broke the spell.

"Eric!" Tania shouted down the stairs. "Jo's here. Let's start."

Tania ran to the door. As she opened it, she announced, "Welcome, Mrs. Helgeson, to the First Annual Fake Music . . ." She stopped in mid-sentence. "Jo!"

Jo stood outside, grinning. She had on a wormy-looking fur stole, a flowered dress that came to mid-calf, and silver slippers. A plastic tiger lily was pinned to her dress.

"Where did you get those silver slippers?" Tania demanded. "Those are exactly like Mrs. Helgeson's, only twice as big."

"Come on, they aren't that big," Jo said. "They're my mom's. Let me in."

Tania moved aside to let in the respected piano

teacher. "OK, but where did you get *that* thing?" She pointed to the fur stole.

"Oh," said Jo, sashaying past like a queen, "just a little something we had lying around . . . at the thrift store. It smells. Don't come too close."

Tania hooted and plugged her nose.

"Time for the festival to begin!" Tania and Jo turned to see Eric, or what must have been Eric beneath a huge green monster mask. The mask had red drips and yellow bumps all over it.

Tania screamed, "Oh, Eric! Gross."

"A perfect judge," Jo said. "Monsterish. He's right. Let the festival begin."

The judge said something that was muffled by his mask.

"What?" Tania and Jo asked together.

Eric lifted up his mask to repeat, "Where's Dodger? He's gotta be the audience."

Tania spotted Dodger under the couch and pulled the reluctant cat out. "Come on, Dodger," she urged. "Just sit on top of the piano and be a good audience."

She set the cat in his usual spot on top of the piano. Dodger settled back on his haunches and looked as if he might cooperate. His tail twitched a little when he saw Eric in the mask, but he didn't move.

"And now," announced the judge, "the very fine, the very wonderful, the best . . ."

"Come *on,* Eric."

" . . . Tania Lindstrom, who will play 'In the Hall of the Mountain Trolls' . . ."

"Mountain *King!*"

"By Mr. Gregg."

"Mr. Grieg," corrected Tania. "*Grieg.*"

Jo flung off her fur stole with a flourish and set it on the couch. "Go to it, dear," she said.

Tania handed her music to the judge. She pulled the bench away from the piano and flipped imaginary coattails up before sitting down.

"Oh that's good, Tania," Jo said, laughing. "Do that on Saturday. They'll die."

Tania began, both arms extended to reach the bass notes. The music crept into the room. As it speeded up, she felt a commotion behind her. Out of the corner of her eye she saw Eric dancing in slow circles.

She decided since this was a fake festival, it was all right if the judge danced a little.

But when the music took off, Eric danced faster, too. Dodger sprang from the piano and hid under the couch.

"Our audience is hiding from the trolls," cried Jo. "Good job, good job, Tania."

Tania kept playing. "Faster!" yelled Eric. "Faster!"

"Don't you think I'm trying?" Tania yelled above the music.

Jo must have tried to pull the cat out from under the couch, because Tania saw Dodger tear across the room, Jo after him. Eric broke out of his circles and joined the chase.

Tania finally gave it up. "Where's everybody going?" She stood up.

Just then, Dodger came skidding around the corner and jumped onto the couch, right onto Mrs. Helgeson's ratty fur stole. The cat hissed and arched his back as if he'd landed on a real fox.

Eric crashed into Jo from behind, and Tania jumped on top of both of them.

The fake music festival ended in a heap of giggles.

Vaudeville

"Tania, do you see that brick building over there?" Grandma Inga asked, pointing out the car window. Tania's mother wound her way through the downtown traffic.

"Is that your old music school?" Tania asked from the back seat.

"No, no, that was where my first apartment was when I came here to study music."

Tania looked. The building stood alone on the block. From the rubble on either side, it looked as if the buildings next to it had been torn down.

"It had a two-burner gas plate, a table, chair, and best of all, a piano. The room was cold, but cheap."

"Did you live there all alone?" Tania asked.

"All alone."

"How old were you?"

"About twenty, I'd say."

"Weren't you sort of . . . lonely?" Tania asked.

Grandma Inga didn't answer for a moment. Then she said, "I had my music, Tania. It was all I wanted."

Tania's mother turned at the next corner.

"There it is," said Grandma Inga.

A large building stood on the corner. The words "Minneapolis Music Conservatory" were cut into the stone with streaks of black beneath each letter.

"It looks exactly the same as it did sixty years ago," Grandma Inga said. "Oh my." She held a gloved hand to her chest.

Tania's mother parked the car.

"Come on. Let's go," said Tania.

She pulled open the heavy front door and saw a long hall. Its polished floor gleamed in the sun that slanted through windows at the far end.

As they walked slowly down the hall, a woman's clear soprano voice filtered out of one of the rooms. Strains of piano music came from another room.

One of the practice-room doors opened, and an old man with a cane walked out, saying good-bye to someone behind him. The piano music grew louder for a moment until the practice-room door shut again.

"Isn't that lovely?" Grandma Inga said to the man, who was passing them. "I just love that piece."

The old man nodded. "Oh yes, but then I'm biased. That's my grandson."

"Fancy that," Grandma Inga said. "I happen to have my . . . say, aren't you . . . "

"Earl Haggen." And then the old man's eyes lit up. "Don't tell me it's you, Inga."

Tania listened to the man and her grandmother

talk about the piano duet they'd played together in Pleasanton fifty years ago. They'd knocked everyone dead, to hear them tell it.

They hadn't seen each other for twenty years, but they talked like best friends. Then Earl Haggen squeezed Grandma Inga's arm and said good-bye.

"Shall we keep walking?" Tania's mother said.

Tania took her grandmother's arm again. "How long did you study here, Grandma?" she asked.

"From January until June, in 1929. Then I ran out of money."

"Half a year? That's all?"

Tania noticed a quick look from her mother. "Half a year of lessons from some of the best musicians in the Midwest would be something to have, don't you think, Tania?"

"Oh, sure," Tania answered. "It's just that I thought she went longer than that."

Because she talked about it so much.

On the second floor, they found what looked like the entrance to an auditorium. Through the darkness Tania could see a stage. Heavy black curtains hung in folds on either side. This must be where the students had their recitals.

Tania found herself wondering what it would be like to play that shiny grand piano with hot stage lights focused on her. Would she wear a red velvet dress? Would she be able to feel the audience, invisible behind the lights?

She broke out into a sudden sweat and shook herself out of her daydream.

"We'd better be going," said Tania's mother. "I don't want you to get too tired, Inga."

"I wish I had the energy I used to," Grandma Inga complained. "Why, we used to do a performance every night at the Orpheum, sometimes two, and then come here for lessons in the morning. I don't know how I did it."

Tania had been walking ahead, but the word "performance" caught her attention. "What performances, Grandma?"

"Oh, the vaudeville shows, Tania. I played the piano in the pit. You know what vaudeville is, don't you?"

Vaudeville. Tania knew the word but not much more. It made her think of clowns and magicians, not good music.

"I didn't know you were in vaudeville," she said.

"How do you suppose I paid the bills here?" Grandma Inga asked, with a sweep of her arm that took in the long hallway. "But then the theater closed and that was that. I went home to Pleasanton."

"I thought you were a soloist, you know, in concerts?"

Tania's mother glanced at her again, but Tania was determined to go on.

"Oh sure," said Grandma Inga. "For lots of groups, community musicals, church concerts, things like that. All my life, even after your grandpa died. But not anymore. Too old."

"Oh."

"Your grandmother is a very accomplished musician, Tania," said her mother. "It's only a very few who go on tour, only a few who see the stage lights."

"I guess." Tania couldn't keep the disappointment from her voice. Why had she thought, all these years, staring at that photograph on the piano, that her grandmother had made it big?

She stopped to watch her grandmother walk slowly down the hall, arm linked with her mother's. And then she knew.

The old woman chatted nonstop as she walked through the school where she had spent only half a year. As if she owned the place.

At dinner that night, Tania pushed her plate away. She didn't know whether she was really sick to her stomach or just angry. One thing she knew for sure. The good mood from the crazy pretend festival with Jo was gone.

Nothing about her grandmother seemed the same anymore. I've looked up to her all these years, Tania thought, and now it seems like I've been looking in the wrong direction.

"I don't feel good, Mom."

"What is it, Tania?" asked her mother. "Your stomach?"

"It muscht be her schtomach," said Eric, his mouth full of potatoes.

"It's nerves," said Grandma Inga. "Tania, you've got to calm down about this festival. You can't play well when you're too tight, you know. The audience will feel it."

"It's not nerves," said Tania. "I bet I have the flu. It's going around." She glared at her napkin to avoid glaring at her grandmother.

Grandma Inga wiped the corners of her mouth and neatly set her napkin in her lap. "We had terrible flu epidemics in Pleasanton way back. Lots of people died from the flu in those days. One year, I had to cut short my first tour with the community chorus and come home to help with the younger ones."

"Did you get the flu, too?" Eric asked.

Grandma Inga shook her head. "A man we knew told us he carried onions in his pocket to ward it off, so I tried it. I didn't get the flu that year. Maybe it was the onions."

"I want to try," Eric said. He jumped up from the table and rustled through a cupboard in the kitchen. He stuck an onion in each pocket and sat down again.

"Do you really think those are going to help you?" Tania asked. As if to make sure they wouldn't, she leaned over and blew on him.

"Tania!" Eric leaned back in his chair so far he nearly fell over.

"I think you'd better get into bed if you've got the flu," said her father.

Tania scraped her chair across the floor and went upstairs. When her mother came up a half-hour later, Tania was lying on her bed.

"Are you feeling better?" her mother asked. "Usually with the flu, the worst part doesn't last long."

Tania didn't answer.

"I know, I know, the worst is yet to come. How could I forget?"

Tania still didn't say anything.

"Did you say Jo was coming to the piano festival? That will be nice for you."

"Yeah."

"Well," said Tania's mother with a sigh. "Let me know if you need anything. You probably shouldn't eat anything else today."

"Mother." Tania propped herself up in bed. "Does Grandma have to stay until the festival? Isn't she getting tired? Wouldn't she rather go back to Arizona?"

"What?"

Tania knew she should quit here, but she didn't. "I don't know, I just wish she wasn't so . . . she seems so much more . . . old-fashioned than she used to be. That sounds dumb."

"I know what you mean," said her mother. "Her health has gone downhill in the past several years. She seems a lot older."

"It's just that I remember her being *fun*," Tania

insisted. "We used to laugh so much when she was around."

Tania paused. "Besides that, she doesn't understand me. And I don't think she's very interested in me or my music. She's just interested in herself."

There. She'd said it.

When her mother didn't answer, Tania could feel her sour thoughts hang in the air like a bad smell.

"Well, you know as well as I do that we can't ask her to leave," her mother said finally. "Just do your best to put up with her, all right? You never know, you might learn something from all those old-fashioned ideas."

"I won't." Tania was sure.

Dress Rehearsal

By the next evening, Tania felt better, but now the weather was unsettled. The wind tossed grainy snow-flakes against the windows for a full-blown spring storm.

Tania pulled on a big purple sweater over her T-shirt and jeans, so she would look more dressed up for the dress rehearsal.

Her father delivered her to Mrs. Helgeson's prim brick house. Its wooden fence had a layer of fresh snow on it.

Tania knocked loudly, then let herself in. Most of the students were already there. Tania joined one of the groups of students and tried to talk away her jitters. After all, this was just a rehearsal.

But Mrs. Helgeson soon herded everyone into the piano room. The grand piano shone like black metal. Hard-backed folding chairs were lined up like soldiers.

Tania took a big breath and sat down.

Mrs. Helgeson made her way toward the piano. Tania watched her. Her teacher's gray hair was always the same length and always curled in exactly the same way. Tania and the other students swore up and down it was a wig.

She was skinny, too, and had pointy elbows, and walked as if she had a board stuck down her back.

But the worst thing was the orchid that Mrs. Helgeson always wore for recitals. The flowers were formal and stiff like her teacher, not warm and flowing like the music.

"All right," Mrs. Helgeson began, and the room immediately grew quiet. "Let's rehearse in the order your names appear in the program. Jay, you're first."

Tania played nearly last. She decided to play her song a little slower than she'd been practicing at home, just to make sure she'd get all the notes right. And when she was finished, she was pleased with herself.

Mrs. Helgeson sat very still. No one else made a sound. Then she said, "Tania, you played all the notes correctly."

Tania waited for the rest.

And it came.

"But it's still not fast enough. This is a wild song, not a funeral march. You've got the king of the mountain trolls threatening Peer Gynt. He's chasing Peer around the castle. That's very dramatic. Show it in the way you play it."

Somehow, Tania knew Mrs. Helgeson wasn't through.

"I think you're being too careful, Tania, because of what happened . . . at Christmas. *Listen* to the music, and let yourself go."

Tania wanted to scream, I've tried! I've tried! Instead, she nodded and said, "OK."

At home that night, Tania stood at her window and looked at the dark outlines of the branches against the newly fallen snow.

If I play it slow enough to get the notes right, she thought, people will think it's a song about dead trolls. If I play it fast enough to make them feel the trolls, I'll mess it up and get lost.

"What am I going to do?" she asked herself out loud.

Someone spoke to her in the darkness.

"You've got to keep at it."

Tania's heart pounded as she whipped around. Behind her, outlined in the light from the hallway, stood her grandmother.

"I'm so sorry," Grandma Inga said. "I didn't mean to scare you. I came to say good night and I heard you talking to yourself."

Tania felt herself blush in the dark.

"You've got to keep at your music, Tania," her grandmother repeated.

"I don't know if I will," Tania admitted. "It's getting so hard."

"Well, what did you expect? To play 'The Spinning Song' in front of family for the rest of your life? You have to move on."

Her harsh words stung Tania.

Neither of them said anything for a minute. And then

her grandmother began again, her words coming slowly.

"Let me tell you something, Tania. I could have been great. I worked terribly hard for it, mind you. And I was good enough. Lots of people told me that. Lord knows, it was all I wanted.

"But there were too many . . . too many things against me. You, Tania. You don't have anything against you."

Now, now, Tania, everything will be all right. The voice in her memory was growing fainter and fainter.

"When you came along, Tania, I knew you had the gift. I told your father he'd better see to it that you got good training."

There was an edge to the old woman's voice that Tania had never heard before. She tried to read her eyes, but the old woman was just a dark silhouette against the light.

What was she saying?

That she wanted Tania to take over where Grandma Inga had left off? That the responsibility to see the stage lights was hers now?

Is that why she had made up songs about acrobatic aardvarks?

Tania couldn't believe that. She didn't want to believe that.

"I'm tired, Grandma," Tania said. And she was.

She knew she could no longer accuse her grandmother of not being interested in her music, but for the first time, her interest felt like a heavy coat on Tania's shoulders.

MidnightConcert

One more day.

Tania practiced hard in the afternoon. She was sure she had never practiced so hard in her life.

By the time she went to bed that night, she was exhausted. She fell asleep with Dodger at her feet.

The sound of piano music from downstairs woke her out of a deep sleep. Tania opened one eye to look at the bright red digits on her clock.

Midnight. Was that Grandma Inga playing? Who else would it be? Her father couldn't play like that. And her mother couldn't find middle C. But why was her grandmother playing in the middle of the night?

She could hear her humming or singing along just as brightly as if it were the middle of the afternoon.

Why didn't somebody go down there and ask her what she was doing? Tania waited, expecting to hear her father's footsteps and polite questions, something like, "Can't sleep, Mother? Isn't it awfully late?"

But Tania heard no footsteps.

Finally, out of curiosity, she threw off the covers and headed downstairs.

She found her grandmother at the piano. The old woman had on a thin robe over her pajamas. The piano lamp was the only light on. It cast long shadows across the room.

Tania waited until her grandmother finished the song, and then in the dim, silent room she asked, "What are you doing, Grandma?"

Things seemed oddly reversed. Last night, it was her grandmother who had interrupted Tania's thoughts.

Grandma Inga didn't even turn around on the bench.

"Am I waking everyone up? You youngsters don't know what it's like not to be able to sleep."

Tania didn't say anything.

"You know, Tania, music helps me remember — and helps me forget. Like this one. I always think of Uncle Karl when I play this."

She started a new song.

"You see," said Grandma Inga when she was finished, "every time he came to visit, he'd play the piano, and that was one of his favorite pieces. He couldn't even speak English, but he was a wonderful musician. Too."

Tania nodded, even though her grandmother wasn't looking at her.

"And this one. It always reminds me of the coyotes on the North Dakota prairie, because once they howled to beat everything when I played it on the clarinet. I think they were imitating it."

She played the piece. And Tania could feel a chill run down her spine. She could almost see coyotes standing on a grassy hill, craning their necks.

When her grandmother was finished, she added, "After that, I played the piece with the sound of those coyotes in my head. And don't you know, someone said to me once, 'Inga, that sounds like a Dakota coyote howling at the moon.' That's when I knew I'd put my own mark on that song."

Grandma Inga turned around to face Tania. "That's what makes someone a good musician — putting your own mark on the music. Do you understand that?"

"I think so," Tania said. "I'm not sure."

The old woman turned back to the piano. "But then, there are those things I'd like to forget. All the work at home. The washing. The cooking.

"And this finger." She paused to examine the finger that had been sewn back on all those years ago.

"I sometimes wonder," she said, "if this finger . . . It's never really had the same flexibility as the rest . . ." Her voice trailed off.

"And there was never enough money for anything . . . not enough money for music school . . ."

Tania interrupted. "Couldn't you borrow some money?"

"I did," her grandmother said. "I borrowed two

hundred dollars from a family friend. But two hundred dollars didn't go very far, even in those days."

It was quiet for a moment. Tania couldn't move.

Then Grandma Inga said, "I think if I couldn't play now, I would scream."

Tania shuddered at her grandmother's words, at the eeriness of the long shadows and the sad mood. She ached for her grandmother, for the struggles, for the lost chances.

No wonder she had never made it big. Who could do anything with all those younger brothers and sisters tagging along like ducklings? Who could do anything besides cook and wash?

"Grandma," she said, "don't you think you should go to bed?"

"I suppose I'm waking everyone up."

"Oh no, don't worry about that. I just thought . . ."

Tania didn't finish. What did she think? If her grandmother went to bed, she wouldn't have such sad thoughts? Is that what she hoped?

Tania went back upstairs.

She curled up under the covers. The music continued.

How long would her grandmother play?

And then it was quiet. But was it? Tania heard a deep bass melody that by now was embedded in her brain. It began slowly and softly, and then gradually picked up speed and rose in pitch.

Her grandmother was playing Tania's festival song.

Tania sat bolt upright in bed.

Why was Grandma Inga doing this? And in the middle of the night? She was playing it far better than Tania ever had. It was like a different song.

Tania seethed. Was her grandmother doing it just to make her mad? Why would she want to make her mad?

The wind rattled her window, and she looked out. She'd forgotten to close the curtains. Against the near-black sky the branches looked threatening, like giant, twisted arms.

She yanked the curtains shut and wheeled around on her bed. With her arms locked tightly around her bent legs, she listened to the music.

As the song grew more furious, Tania began to feel something at her back, like the sensation of someone standing too close.

That's ridiculous, she thought.

But the sensation remained. The hairs on her neck bristled. Was it the mischief in the music that was making her skin prickle? Or was it those giant, twisted arms reaching toward her?

The music built and built toward its climax. Tania had never heard it played so powerfully. She squeezed her eyes shut and wavered somewhere between utter pleasure and utter terror.

At the final crashing notes of the song, she couldn't stand it any longer. She jerked around and pulled her

curtains open, half expecting to see a treeful of trolls reaching out to snatch her.

Inga, watch out for the trolls hiding in the back. They'll grab you if you sing sour.

Everything looked the same, but she knew the trolls were out there. They'd waited backstage for her grandmother, and they were waiting in this tree for her.

Just then, the wind knocked a slice of snow off a branch. Tania watched it fall.

I know they're out there, she thought, but I'm not going to let them get me. I'm not even going to fall off the stage like Grandma did.

It was some time before Tania fell back to sleep in the dead quiet of the house.

Saturday

The Festival

Tania woke up cold. Last night's eerie mood and prickly fear were still with her. She put on a T-shirt, a turtleneck sweater, a jumper, a vest, and tights, and still she had goose bumps.

Downstairs, she sat at the table and peeled a banana slowly and deliberately.

I'm going to make it.

I'm going to make it.

I want to make it.

She ate the banana and announced, "I'm walking there."

"Me, too," Eric declared. "I want to walk, too." He ran for his jacket and his boots.

"Go ahead," said Tania's mother. "We'll bring your music. I'm not sure why you want to do this."

Tania didn't answer, but she was hoping the exercise would melt the bone-deep chill she felt.

The late-March sun splashed cool light through the window onto the gray walls. It was here, in the basement of a university building, that Tania would play in the piano festival.

Despite climbing up and down a mile's worth of snowbanks, she was still cold.

Mrs. Helgeson arrived. There was the orchid.

Jo finally strode through the door in jeans and sneakers. No one could make her wear a dress, and no amount of snow could make her wear boots.

Tania dragged Jo with her to the bathroom so she could run her stiff, cold hands under hot water. It helped. Then they sat down on chairs in front of Tania's family and waited.

But Tania couldn't concentrate on the performances of the students before her. She felt distant from the room, from her own body. Suddenly her name was called.

She stood up, knees shaking. Tania handed her sheet music to the judge. He looked it over, then nodded.

She sat down at the piano and turned her attention to the row of eighty-eight black and white keys in front of her.

Tania began to play "In the Hall of the Mountain King." Her fingers barely touched the keys, as if each key were boiling hot. The music bounced off the bare walls of the room and sent back ripples of mischief.

Tania shivered, partly because she was still cold. But fear was sharpening her senses, and she recognized this mischief swirling around her.

I remember, she thought. I remember.

Last night's energy and emotion flooded into her. The black and white piano keys began to blur into the gray of a city sky at night. The music carried her back to her bedroom window, back to the oak tree.

In her mind, she saw buds emerging from the lower tree branches.

But were they buds?

Instead of pale green and soft, they were brown and misshapen, the curse of a cold spring.

And they weren't buds. They were trolls.

Freed by the creeping bass notes of the music, the ugly troll-buds unfolded like leaves and crept up the tree's black and twisted branches.

More troll-buds popped out from the branches, and they, too, climbed the tree, faster and faster, like the hot notes on the page.

The trolls spread like licks of flame into the upper branches. The tree swayed, its branches bowed.

Suddenly trolls were everywhere on every branch, and the tree was full of trolls. They scampered toward the top, toward Tania's window, toward Tania. The tree shook. The ground shook.

The trolls reached out from a thousand branches, closer and closer, closer and closer.

Suddenly there was a crash, and the trolls fell harmlessly from the branches like leaves. They drifted gently to the ground.

The music stopped.

The trolls and the tree disappeared.

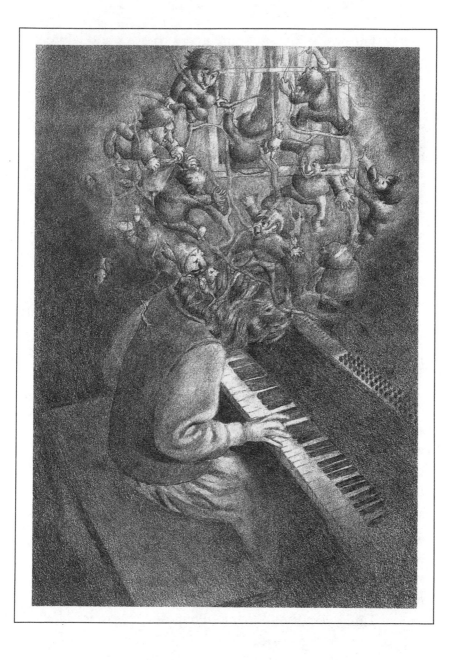

The gray of the sky separated into black and white. Eighty-eight black and white piano keys.

But the crashing noise remained. It rang in Tania's ears.

The room was bursting in an explosion of applause.

Sweat dripped into Tania's eye, and her layers of clothes stuck to her sweaty body. She'd done it. She'd really done it. She smiled and stood up to bow to the audience, to *her* audience.

"I think you forgot all about me," Jo whispered, grinning, when Tania returned to her seat. "You were too busy chasing trolls."

Tania wiped the sweat from her forehead and grinned back. She'd not only forgotten about Jo, she'd forgotten about everyone else in the audience.

The music helps me remember and helps me forget.

But Jo was wrong. Tania knew she hadn't been *chasing* trolls. She'd been escaping them. And they weren't her grandmother's trolls. They were her own trolls.

After the last student had played, everyone stood around waiting for the written comments. Her mother and father hugged Tania over and over.

Mrs. Helgeson beamed. "Your interpretation was . . . was . . ." — her eyes searched the folding chairs for the right word — ". . . unique!" she declared.

Tania laughed. Mrs. Helgeson's orchid had slipped, and hung upside down.

"I'm glad you're done with that one," Eric said. "I've heard it a million times."

A woman handed a piece of paper to Tania, who handed it immediately to Jo. "You read it," she demanded, and took a big breath.

" 'Rhythm good,' " read Jo, " 'memorization excellent; notes missed because of the fast tempo; interpretation inspiring.' Does that mean they liked it?"

Jo paused, then added, "Oh, here it says at the bottom, 'You stamped this piece Tania.' "

Tania blew out her breath. "They said that? Just like that?"

That's what makes someone a good musician — putting your own mark on the music.

"I did miss a few notes," Tania admitted.

"Well, *I* didn't notice," Jo said. "So . . . are you going to quit piano?"

Tania grinned. "I guess not."

She studied the judge's comments for a minute, until she realized that the room had grown quiet. At the same time, she realized that her grandmother hadn't spoken to her since her performance. Where was she? Maybe she hadn't liked it.

Tania's heart sank.

She looked around and saw that her family and Jo were already outside in the hall, chatting. But where was her grandmother?

She found her sitting at the grand piano. It had attracted her like a magnet. Grandma Inga was staring at the keys, lightly brushing them with her fingers, as if a heavier touch would harm them.

"You beat the dickens out of those trolls, Tania. And you didn't even fall off the stage. Good for you."

Tania smiled with relief. Her grandmother knew. Of course she would know.

"Thanks," Tania croaked, her voice hoarse. She could feel the heavy coat lifting from her shoulders.

Grandma Inga began playing, softly at first. It was not enough to pull anyone back into the room, but it was enough to keep Tania. She sat down to listen.

She heard her grandmother play a song that she had heard many times before. Nothing special.

That wasn't all she heard. She heard a plucky three-year-old child performing onstage.

She heard a young girl learning to play the piano again with a stitched-up finger.

She heard a proud young woman practicing the piano alone in a cold apartment.

Her grandmother played for a long time, often with her eyes closed. And after a while, Tania closed hers, too. For some reason, with her eyes closed, she found it easier to see.